Kuskowski, Alex.
Down and out /

c2012.
33305223646989
la   03/08/12

DOWN AND OUT

Alex Kuskowski

SADDLEBACK
EDUCATIONAL PUBLISHING

DISTRICT ⑬

SADDLEBACK
EDUCATIONAL PUBLISHING
www.sdlback.com

Copyright © 2012 by Saddleback Educational Publishing
All rights reserved. No part of this book may be
reproduced in any form or by any means, electronic or
mechanical, including photocopying, recording, scanning,
or by any information storage and retrieval system
without the written permission of the publisher.

ISBN-13: 978-1-61651-582-9
ISBN-10: 1-61651-582-1
eBook: 978-1-61247-247-8

Printed in Guangzhou, China
0511/05-16-11

16 15 14 13 12   1 2 3 4 5

1

Terrance looked at the clock. It was almost closing time. No one was in the corner store. He sighed. Couldn't he close early?

The door opened.

"Think fast, fool!" Someone threw something. Terrance caught it. It was a football.

Terrance turned and glared. It was Darius. Wasn't school enough?

This guy just wouldn't leave him alone.

"What ya want, Darius?" Terrance asked.

Darius grabbed ten candy bars. "Didn't think you'd catch that. I heard you were slow. Maybe it's just math."

Terrance's face got hot. Mr. Fisher called on him in class today. Terrance couldn't answer the problem.

Terrance was failing math. Well, not yet. He would be soon. He hated that everyone knew. Especially Jasmine. She probably thought he was dumb.

Darius tossed some money on the counter. "Better check your change. Seein' as how you can't add. Later, loser." Darius took the football. He left.

Terrance swore. He counted the money. Darius hadn't paid enough. What a jerk.

Someone said, "Hey, man! Don't be usin' fool words 'round your sisters, T."

Terrance smiled. It was Miguel. He came in with Terrance's twin sisters, Jacinta and Adrianna. They were eight years old. "Hey, Miguel. Hey, A. and J."

The girls hugged Terrance. Then they ran around the shelves. They liked to play tag in the store. They never sat still.

"Don't knock anything!" Terrance yelled.

"I saw Darius leaving," Miguel said. "He was coming out of here. Dude bothering ya?"

"Naw, man. Guy's a jerk. Nothing I can't handle." Terrance shrugged.

"Right. You let me know. You up for some soccer after this?" Miguel was a soccer star. Terrance wasn't very good at soccer. He was better at football.

"How 'bout we toss the football around instead?" Terrance suggested.

"Okay, man. Call me when you're done here." Miguel headed out. The girls followed at a sprint.

Terrance watched them go. He saw something on the street. It was a white van. It was parked there when Terrance started work. Some guys were around it. They watched the store.

Terrance closed the store. Those guys were just goofin'. He wouldn't worry.

2

Terrance stared at the problem. He didn't know the answer. Was it $a + b$ or $a \times b$?

He thought about throwing the football with Miguel last night. It was fun. He threw it half the block. Miguel was impressed. Terrance wished he could play football more.

Mr. Fisher called on him. "Want to try solving it, Wright?"

Terrance shook his head. He heard Darius whisper, "Wright? How 'bout wrong!"

The kids in the class laughed. Terrance stretched his legs. He ignored them. But he didn't know the answer.

Behind him, Darius laughed. "Big and dumb. What a combo."

Terrance clenched his fists. He hated being big. He hated Darius. "One more word, Darius, an' I'm gonna bust your grill," Terrance thought.

Darius said, "I bet Jasmine likes me 'cause I know how to add."

Terrance stood up. He turned around. He was going to hit Darius this time.

Mr. Fisher got between the two boys. "Okay. That's enough. No need to get overworked. It's math. It'll be here tomorrow."

The bell rang. Everyone stood up. Terrance grabbed his bag. He couldn't wait to get out of there.

"Not you, Terrance." Terrance sat back down. He was in trouble.

"I know I'm just the football coach. I'll only be here until Ms. Rooney gets back. But Terrance? I know you're smarter than this."

Terrance was confused. Man, Mr. Fisher was pushy. What did he want?

Mr. Fisher continued, "Terrance, I know you can do better. Maybe a tutor …"

"What? Like for idiots?" Terrance stood up. "I'm not stupid." He walked out of class.

Mr. Fisher said, "Terrance, wait. Just give it a try." Terrance just kept walking.

Terrance sat next to Miguel at lunch. He told him what Mr. Fisher said.

"A tutor isn't a bad idea," Miguel said. Terrance ignored him. He opened his sack lunch.

"Don't ya know who your tutor would be? Don't you?" Miguel asked. He grinned.

"You?" Terrance said. Miguel got good grades. Better than Terrance. Maybe getting help from Miguel wouldn't be too bad.

"No, fool. Jasmine," Miguel said. "She's the math tutor.

Terrance bit into his sandwich. Studying with Jasmine? He'd have an excuse. He could talk to her.

He'd give tutoring a shot.

3

"Hi, Terrance." Jasmine walked into the math room. She sat down next to Terrance.

Terrance smiled. "Hi, Jasmine." He couldn't stop staring at her.

"Ready to get started?" She pulled out her math book.

Terrance frowned. He'd forgotten. That's why he was here. To study math.

"Oh, right," he said. Terrance got his book out too.

Jasmine could see he was worried. "Come on. Be easy," she said. "I got this for ya. I promise." Jasmine smiled at him.

Jasmine's smile was pretty fly. She was one of the hottest chicks in school. On the dance team *and* smart. Would she ever go for him? Not if he was dumb.

Jasmine opened her book. She started explaining a math problem. Terrance looked at her long, black braid.

"See? It's easy. You know a and b. So you can get c!" she said. Or something. Terrance tried to concentrate.

"Stop movin'! You're making the table shake," Jasmine said. Papers fell on the floor.

Terrance was embarrassed. He couldn't sit still. Jasmine made it worse. She was so nice. He wanted to impress her. But he didn't know how. "Sorry," he said.

"It's okay. I gotta go anyway." She picked up the papers. "Dance practice. Here's Mr. Fisher. He'll help you."

"Sorry, Jasmine," Terrance said again.

"See you later!" She ran off. At least she didn't seem mad.

"Hey, Wright. What's got you?" Mr. Fisher took Jasmine's seat. He had a football.

"Nothing, Mr. Fisher." Terrance got up.

"Son, I know you been having problems. Don't try to fix them all at once. You know what helps me? Getting that energy out. You've got to find something to work for. Come on outside with me."

"What? Now, Mr. Fisher?" Terrance was lost.

"Yes. Now, Mr. Wright." Some people thought Mr. Fisher was weird. Terrance never thought so. Until now.

When they were outside, Mr. Fisher began throwing the football to Terrance. Terrance didn't know what was going on. But he liked throwing the ball.

Soon he relaxed. They played catch for an hour. By the end Mr. Fisher was tired.

"You're pretty good, Wright. I want you to try out."

"What for?"

"The football team! What else could I be talkin' about, son?"

4

Terrance couldn't stop thinking about Mr. Fisher. He gave Terrance a playbook. Terrance read it at work.

He remembered when he played football. The helmets knocking in a play. The smell of the grass during the game. Running till he dropped. Terrance loved it all.

He stopped playing when his dad left. His mom worried he would get hurt. He didn't want to complain. Make things harder for her. But he missed football. Terrance looked back at the playbook.

He forgot about school, Jasmine, everything. Even the van across the street. At least till he walked by it after work. The guys blew smoke in his face.

Terrance was bigger. But there were more of them. He kept walking home.

Terrance dragged his feet to his apartment. His mom and Sid were in the living room. Sid was his mom's boyfriend.

Terrance told them what Mr. Fisher said. "I want to join the football team, Ma. Please."

"Too dangerous," his mom said. "Besides, that was your father's thing. Now you have Sid."

Sid was okay. He was good to Terrance's mom. He and Terrance didn't talk much, though.

Sid owned five stores. One of them was the store where Terrance worked. That's how Terrance's mom met him.

Pretty soon Sid moved in. He helped pay the bills. Something his dad never did.

Terrance did not like the store. He'd gotten the job after his dad left. To help out his mom. Now maybe he didn't need to work anymore.

Sid said, "Honey, why not let him play ball? I've been thinking 'bout hiring someone else at the store. Let Terrance be a kid."

Terrance was surprised. But he quickly said, "Yeah, Ma. Please? I don't wanna work at the store no more. It's freakin' me out. I'll even study real hard."

Sid looked at him. "What do you mean? What's freaking you out?"

Terrance didn't know what to say. "It's just this van of guys. They keep hanging. It's nothing."

Sid got up. He took Terrance into the kitchen. "It's not nothing. Is it a white van?"

Terrance nodded.

"Remember last month? My store on Grand got robbed. There was a white van. Call me if they show up again. Ever. I'll help you out with your mom. Just don't tell her about this. Okay?"

Terrance nodded again. He could keep his mouth shut. If he could play football. No problem.

5

Terrance had waited for this. He felt the grass under his fingers. The wind picked up. Mr. Fisher's whistle blew. Now he was Coach Fisher. Terrance lunged across the line.

Thwack! He took down the quarterback. It took one swipe. He helped him back up.

Coach Fisher's whistle blew again. "Like the energy, Wright!

Keep it together. And don't injure my quarterback!"

Let Coach yell. Terrance didn't care. He was playing again!

They lined up. This time Terrance felt the hit. He struggled back. His arms ached. He held himself up. He wouldn't give up.

His face dripped. They ran for an hour. Then they lifted weights. They did drills over and over. Terrance forgot how hard football was. It was still better than work. Way better.

On the field he didn't worry. Not about math. Or the van. Or tutoring.

He thought of Jasmine. Maybe if he played football …

Glonk! Terrance's head hit the ground. It was a hard tackle.

Coach Fisher was yelling. "Come on, son! Where was that play, team? Run it again."

"Can't keep up, huh?" It was Darius. Terrance forgot Darius was on the team.

"Ain't nobody askin' for your two cents." Terrance had been having a good time.

Darius said, "Really. I been scopin' this girl. Her body be blazin' hot!"

"Shut up, Darius. You ain't got nothing." Darius was lying.

"Not yet. But listen, fool," Darius said. "You'd better step off. Jasmine is my girl. You're too dumb. Always were. Always will be. Ain't no football changing that."

Terrance almost stood up. But the whistle blew. He blocked the guy in front of him instead. Hard.

He didn't say anything. Football might not be so easy after all.

6

Miguel met Terrance at the end of practice. He grabbed a football.

"Hey, Terrance!" Miguel threw the ball. The thing was sad. It wobbled in the air. Terrance had no trouble catching it. He threw it back.

"Oof!" Miguel caught it. But just barely.

Terrance laughed. "Maybe you should stick to soccer, bro."

"Don't hate. I got this." Miguel threw the ball back. It was better this time. "Since you made the team last week you been all football all the time. Let's head home. We gotta study. You gotta study."

"Naw, man. I been doing better. Thanks to Jasmine. Math is easier each day." Terrance grinned. He really liked being tutored by her. They met most days during study hall.

Miguel and Terrance walked down the street. A white van drove by. Terrance jolted. Another store had been robbed. It was on the news last night. Someone was stabbed. It wasn't Sid's store. But Terrance was worried.

"Yo. You never told me what's up with that. Seems she be crushing on you," Miguel said.

Terrance forgot the van. "For real? I hope so. I asked her to the dance."

Terrance acted cool. Like he hadn't been nervous to ask. He thought about it all week. Today he finally asked her.

"What'd she say? You gotta tell a bro," Miguel said. "I'm going with Lexi. She's friends with Jasmine. Maybe we can double."

"Jasmine said she was planning on going with her girls but … She's thinkin' about it." A maybe was better than a no right? Terrance hoped so.

"Aw, man! You're in." Miguel punched his arm. "She told Darius to back up off her yesterday when he asked. He was steamed. You better watch him, bro."

"No way! She blew him off?" Terrance was surprised. He thought maybe that's why she hadn't said yes. That she was going with Darius.

"Yeah. You gotta tell that dude to stop talking smack to you. His head's up his ass anyway."

Terrance shook his head. "I don't know, man."

"Seriously," Miguel said. "You think a Mexican in this 'hood never had haters? Just stand up to him. He'll back down. Bullies always do. Can't take their own medicine."

Terrance hoped it would be that easy. He'd see what happened at the next practice.

7

Terrance cracked his knuckles. He finished the test. He'd studied for two weeks. He looked at his answers. He could hear Jasmine in his head. "It's easy," she said.

Jasmine was wrong. It wasn't easy. His palms were sweaty. He forgot equations. He thought of the game next week. It was all anyone talked about.

He'd filled out the answers, though. They weren't guesses. He could pass this test. He knew it.

He handed the test to Ms. Rooney. Coach Fisher was done subbing. Terrance was the last one to leave the room.

"Good luck, Mr. Wright," Ms. Rooney said.

Which was she talking about? Football or the test? Terrance couldn't tell. He didn't ask. He had to get to the football field. Extra practice for the game.

On the field, they practiced tackles. Coach set up a play. Terrance was the right defensive tackle. He had to get the quarterback. Darius was on the offensive line.

Darius led the trash talk. "Terrance got a body like a Coke bottle. Boy can't walk. Can't play ball. Can't barely talk. Can't add that honey up."

Coach blew the whistle. Terrance ignored the quarterback. He went straight for Darius.

Terrance drove him to the ground. "Shut the hell up, Darius!" Terrance got up. The play was over.

"Man, you best be risin' up off me! I ain't never done nothing." Darius jumped up. He pushed Terrance.

"You been talking smack about me. And Jasmine." Terrance grabbed Darius' helmet. He got right in his face. "I don't want to mess you up. So lay off," Terrance said.

Terrance let go. He felt good. No one was going to walk over him.

Coach Fisher made Terrance do push-ups. It didn't matter. Darius was quiet for once.

8

Today Terrance didn't mind working. It was his last day. The new guy was going to start tomorrow. Sid had kept his word.

Everything was good. No one was in the store. His sisters playing tag didn't count.

The math test had gone okay. He was going to pass. He studied really hard for it. Harder than for any other test. He stood up to Darius today too!

Terrance turned up the radio. He started stocking the shelves. Terrance watched his sisters play. He put cans on the shelf.

He thought about football. He was sore from practice. That was good. Coach Fisher said his blocks were better. He'd get to play in the game!

Coach Fisher was right about football. You've got to have something to work for. It makes you work at everything.

He was right about math too. Terrance knew now not to try to do it all at once. He also knew having a tutor wasn't a bad thing. Especially since his tutor was Jasmine. He liked her more each time.

Terrance looked up from the shelf. He saw it out of the corner of his eye. The white van was back.

Terrance wasn't sure what to do. Sid said to call him. Other stores had been robbed. Someone had been stabbed! Terrance didn't want that to happen here.

He kept stocking. He pretended not to see the van. He pulled out his phone. He called Sid's cell.

The phone rang. It rang again. Terrance was worried. Would Sid pick up?

"What do you want?" It was Sid. He sounded busy. Terrance hoped he wasn't too far away.

"Yo, Sid? It's Terrance. That white van is back. The girls are here too. I don't think it's a deal but …"

"What!" Sid was paying attention now. "I'll be right there. Hold tight. I'm calling the cops."

"I don't think …" Terrance started. The phone clicked off. The cops were coming? What if Terrance was wrong? How would he explain?

"Jacinta and Adrianna! You need to go home. Now!" Terrance yelled. His sisters didn't hear. The music was too loud.

The door jingled. Someone came in. Terrance called out, "I'll be right there."

He walked around the aisle. He almost ran into the customer. It was a man from the white van. He didn't say anything. Terrance knew something was wrong.

Jacinta peeked around the shelf. She screamed. Terrance saw it too. The man had a knife!

9

Terrance froze. He didn't know what to do. What if his sisters got hurt? He couldn't let that happen.

Adrianna ran around the corner. She fell into a stand of chips. They went flying.

The man turned. He moved toward the noise.

Terrance knew it had to be now. He didn't think. He did the tackle

Coach Fisher drilled them on. The man went down. Terrance grabbed the knife. The man kicked Terrance. He tried to punch him.

Terrance heard sirens. He saw flashing lights. The police were here! The man jumped away. He was out the door. He ran down the street.

Terrance saw the police chase him. They would catch him. More police surrounded the van. They arrested the other guys.

Terrance forgot about them. He looked for his sisters.

"Jacinta? Adrianna? That guy is gone. You okay?" The girls came out from the aisle. Adrianna had a small bruise from the chip stand. Jacinta was not hurt.

The worst damage was to the chips. Terrance joked it was a "chip catastrophe." The girls giggled.

One of the cops came into the store. He asked Terrance what happened. Terrance told him. He gave the cop the knife.

The cop said Terrance would have to go to the station. He needed to make a statement. But it didn't have to be today.

Adrianna told the cop about the chip stand. Jacinta told him how Terrance had saved them.

Soon Sid showed up. Terrance was so glad to see him! Sid talked to the cops for a few minutes.

Then Sid came over to Terrance. He and the girls were at the counter.

It was covered with chip bags. Terrance could barely see Sid over them.

Sid came around the counter. He hugged the girls. "Are you two okay?" he asked. "I got here as fast as I could!"

"We're good as long as we get chips!" Jacinta yelled.

"Yeah. And Terrance gets double! He was so brave! He saved the store," Adrianna said.

Jacinta added, "He stood up to the bad guy. For us!"

Sid said, "I'm proud of you, Terrance. You did good, son." He slapped Terrance on the shoulder. "Well, the store's closed for today. Let's go home."

Terrance had to admit it. Hearing Sid's praise felt as good as standing up for himself.

10

It was halftime. They were winning 24 to 10. Terrance waited on the sidelines. He jumped to keep his muscles warm. He had bruises on his bruises. It didn't matter. He was playing in a real game!

He was on the line in the first half. It was more exciting than practice. He loved it! He played well too. He even sacked the quarterback once! Coach Fisher said he could start the second half.

The halftime show ended. The crowd cheered. The dance team left the field. Terrance watched Jasmine sprint off the field. She came right over to him.

"Hey, Jasmine. You were … uh, great out there." Terrance winced. He'd been a hero for a week. Everyone heard about the robbery. He was on TV! He still couldn't talk smooth to Jasmine.

"You weren't so bad either. Your tackles looked good. Nobody got by you!"

Terrance smiled. He felt proud. She'd been watching him! His bruises hurt a little less.

"How did you do on the test? I never heard. Still need a tutor?" Jasmine asked.

Terrance forgot to tell her! "I got a B-minus." Terrance was proud of that too. It was one of his best grades all year.

"But I'll still need a tutor," he quickly said. "Can't let my grades slip. Not now I'm on the team." What if she didn't want to?

"Ten seconds, team! On the field!" Coach Fisher yelled.

"How 'bout a date to the dance?" Jasmine talked fast. "Still need one of those? I heard some girls been asking you."

Terrance's cheeks got warm. He told all the other girls no. He liked

Jasmine a lot. He only wanted to go with her.

"Wright! Get on the field! *Now!*" Coach Fisher yelled. The second half was starting. But Terrance had to know.

"You going with your girls?" he asked Jasmine.

Jasmine smiled. "Nope," she said. "They all got dates. After I said I was going with you."

Terrance smiled back at Jasmine. She gave him a quick hug.

Terrance sprinted onto the field. He set up on the defensive line. He waited for the snap. He couldn't stop grinning.

He thought about how good this week had been. Passing the test.

Standing up to Darius. Being a hero. Playing in the game. It had all been good. Really good. But now it was great.